MR. COOL

Roger Hargreaves

Written and illustrated by
Adam Hargreaves

EGMONT

Poor Jack Robinson wasn't feeling very well.

He had been in bed for days and he had to stay in bed until he was better.

"I'm bored," he huffed. "I wish I could go outside and play with my friends."

Suddenly, a blue blur shot in through the open window.

It looped-the-loop around the light in the ceiling and a small blue figure, wearing a hat, landed on the end of Jack's bed.

"Cool!" said Jack.

"That's me. Mr Cool," said Mr Cool.

"Cool!" repeated Jack.

"You look a bit bored," said Mr Cool. "I thought we could go and have some fun."

"I wish I could," said Jack, "but I'm not allowed out of bed."

"I think we could make an exception just this once," said Mr Cool, and he clicked his fingers.

The next instant, Jack found himself sitting in the cockpit of a jet aeroplane.

"Why don't you take it out for a spin?" suggested Mr Cool.

"What? Can I really fly it?" said Jack.

"Sure you can!" said Mr Cool. "It's easy!"

So Jack flew the jet-plane out across the Atlantic Ocean and back.

"That was cool," cried Jack, when they were back on the ground. "Thanks, Mr Cool!"

"We haven't finished yet," said Mr Cool, and he clicked his fingers again.

Jack heard a crowd roar. He was at a football ground, but he wasn't sitting in the crowd. He was on the bench with the other players!

And he was even wearing the team strip!

"Quick!" said Mr Cool. "The manager wants you to go on."

"He wants me to play?" said Jack, incredulously. "But they're Capital United!"

And you'll never guess what … Jack scored the winning goal

"Wow! That was so cool!" said Jack.

As Jack walked off the pitch, Mr Cool clicked his fingers, and whisked them away …

… to climb the tallest tree in the world!

He clicked his fingers again and, before you could say "Jack Robinson", …

… they were standing on top of a mountain!

"Where are we?" called Jack, over the noise of the wind.

"Mount Everest!" said Mr Cool.

"How cool! What are we doing here?" shouted Jack.

"Sledging!" said Mr Cool. "Let's go!"

Jack and Mr Cool slid from the very top to the very bottom of Mount Everest.

"That was the coolest thing ever!" cried Jack.

"It was more like the c … c … coldest," stuttered Mr Cool.

For the final time that day, Mr Cool clicked his fingers.

In an instant, Jack found himself back in his bedroom.

"Thank you so much, Mr Cool," said Jack.
"That was …"

"… amazing?!" laughed Mr Cool.

"Well, I'll be off," said Mr Cool. "But there's one more thing, Jack. Have a look in the mirror."

With this, Mr Cool shot out through the open window.

Jack went into the bathroom, and looked in the mirror.

"Cool!" said Jack when he saw himself.

And why do you think Jack was so pleased?

That's right, all his spots had gone. Jack was better.

I wonder, on which page did Jack get better?